W9-CAJ-992

Whiting Public Library
Whiting, Indiana

AMERICA'S
TEST KITCHEN

Peyton Picks _the_ Perfect Pie

A Thanksgiving Celebration

Story by Jack Bishop

Illustrations by Michelle Mee Nutter

Whiting Public Library
Whiting, Indiana

Peyton is particular. But she's not picky. Grown-ups use that word a lot.
Picky. Picky. Picky. It's never a good thing. And it's not fair.
Peyton likes dogs *and* cats, scooters *and* bikes, pools *and* beaches.
She's not picky. Peyton likes to try new things.

She learned all about long division in math class. It was hard at first, but now it's fun. Like solving a puzzle.

Peyton just started playing the saxophone. She remembers to practice every day and enjoys it—as long as her dog Mila doesn't howl.

And Peyton loves sports. Every sport. Peyton even likes dodgeball. And who likes dodgeball?

But Peyton is particular about food.

She doesn't like it when
two foods touch on her plate.

She doesn't like green foods.
Or orange foods.
Or red foods.

Peyton doesn't like foods that
are gooey or gummy, sticky
or slimy, frosted or flaky.

And she most definitely
doesn't like chunky or
lumpy foods.

But lately Peyton has been thinking a lot about food.
Her parents, Penny and Peter, love to cook. They never say it, but Peyton wonders
if they would like her to be, well, less *particular* about food.

Peyton's parents host Thanksgiving each year and ask guests to bring pies. Everyone is always so happy during the holiday, surrounded by people they love and food they enjoy. Not Peyton, though. She loves her family, but the food is so green . . . so lumpy . . . and so flaky.

"I'm going to change this year," Peyton tells Mila. "I'm going to try all the food."

Mila gives Peyton a quizzical look.

"OK, OK, not *all* the food," says Peyton with a shudder, thinking about the lumpy gravy. "How about I try one new thing?" Peyton hears her mother singing as she rolls out pie dough. "I'll try PIE!" Peyton exclaims.

On Thanksgiving morning, Peyton helps her mom weave strips of pie dough into a pretty top.

"The small holes allow juices from the apples to evaporate," Penny says. "That's why my crust is so flaky."

Peyton tries to pretend she didn't just hear the word "flaky."

She looks over at her dad. "Dad, do YOU need any help?"

The first guests are here. It's Uncle Sherwood and Uncle Mark.
Peyton is excited—and a little nervous—to see all the different pies.

"We've brought our famous lemon chess
pie," says Uncle Mark.

"I like checkers better than chess," Peyton whispers to Mila. Then she
asks her uncles, "What does this pie have to do with playing chess?"

Uncle Sherwood is a history buff. "This recipe dates back several hundred years to England. The original name was cheese pie because the yellow filling sets up very firm, like a piece of cheese."

"Cheese in the pie?" Peyton is concerned. That sounds both lumpy and sticky.

"Don't worry," says Uncle Mark reassuringly. "There's no cheese in our pie—just lemon, sugar, cornmeal, butter, and eggs."

When the next guest arrives, Peyton is in the kitchen. She runs to hug Maria Alvarez, a social studies teacher at Peyton's school.

"Peyton, don't crush my ruffled milk pie!"

"Ruffled what?!" Peyton asks her favorite teacher.

"I first had this pie in Greece," explains Ms. Alvarez. "It's made with thin sheets of phyllo dough that are shaped into ruffles. A sweetened egg custard is poured over the phyllo, and the pie is baked until the phyllo is crisp and the custard just wiggles."

"Oh no," Peyton whispers to Mila. "A pie that wiggles . . . And aren't ruffles for dresses?"

Peyton opens the front door to find a crowd on the porch. It's Grandma Pearl, Grandpa Rich, Aunt Mia, Uncle Noah, and Peyton's three cousins—Jude, Jane, and Jamal.

"Make room for me and my millionaire pie," says Grandma Pearl.

Peyton asks her grandmother, "Do I get extra allowance if I try a piece?"

"Don't be silly, Peyton. But this pineapple pie does taste like a million bucks."

"Don't tell your parents," she adds, "but I bought my pie at the bakery for $10. What a deal!"

There's a knock at the back door. Peyton and Mila run to greet the next-door neighbors.

"Bonjour, Peyton," says Mrs. Macaron. "Please take my plum galette."
"Ga-let?" asks Peyton.

"Oui, Peyton," exclaims Madeleine, who is in Peyton's grade. "A galette is a rustic French tart. You arrange sliced plums on the dough, fold over the edges, and bake. And voilà!"

"Don't forget the candied violets,"
adds Mr. Macaron. "Or your mother's
cinnamon whipped cream."

Peyton looks over to Mila and says,
"Flowers made into candies? Whipped
cream with cinnamon? Finding a
plain pie is going to be harder than
I thought."

Cousins Rachel and Russell from New York
have brought Boston cream pie.

Peyton is confused.
They aren't from Boston, and
their pie looks like a cake.

Aunt Grace has a tray of whoopie pies. They look like chocolate flying saucers held together by a creamy white filling. Peyton likes the name. And she likes chocolate. But she wonders, "Is it cheating to try a pie that looks like a gigantic cookie?"

The Patels from across town arrive with Mississippi mud pie. Peyton can finally spell Mississippi correctly, but mud doesn't sound good.

Peyton hears a honk on the street. It's the Lees and their twin baby girls. They have brought two pies: pumpkin pecan and cranberry pear. "These pies sound twice as fancy and twice as scary," Peyton thinks.

Peyton goes back into the kitchen.
Maybe her parents can offer some advice
about choosing the right pie.
But Peyton's parents are VERY busy.

Peyton's dad asks her to carry some dishes
to the table and then turns to Penny.
"We're missing someone. Where is your sister?"

"Polly texted to say she's running late. An ice storm in Denver meant her plane was diverted to Dallas. Polly said to start without her."

At the table, Peyton takes two slices of turkey. White meat, of course, and no skin.
And no thanks to lumpy gravy. A fluffy roll sits next to—but not touching—the turkey.
She adds a tidy scoop of mashed potatoes.

Penny gently clinks a fork against the side of her glass and the guests quiet down.
"Peter, Peyton, and I are so grateful that you all could share this special day with us.
We celebrate with food, but having you all around our table is the real treat."

It's finally pie time.

There are big ones and small ones, tall ones and short ones, red ones and yellow ones, and . . . is that even a green one?

Peyton has never seen so many pies!
But one thing they all have in common,
Peyton thinks, is that they're kind of
lumpy and maybe a little bit sticky or flaky.

"I'm not sure I can do this,"
Peyton confides to Mila.
Just then the doorbell rings.

Aunt Polly strides into the house holding two large, frosty containers.
"I didn't bake pie!" she calls out, laughing.
"I brought something even better. Ice cream!"

"I didn't know you could put ice cream on pie," Peyton says.
"Of course you can," Polly says. "It's called pie à la mode.
The truth is, pie is just OK. But add ice cream, and pie is divine!"

Peyton is suddenly feeling braver. She likes ice cream.
Particularly vanilla ice cream. Peyton takes a bite of
her mom's apple pie. The pie is a little lumpy. And a
little flaky. But it doesn't seem as scary.

Peyton takes another bite.
Then another.
"I thought I didn't like pie.
But I guess I do."

"Sometimes when
we think we don't
like something, we
just have to look at
it in a different way,"
says her wise aunt.
"If all else fails, just
add ice cream."

"I like your apple pie, Mom," says Peyton. Penny looks surprised. Happy, but surprised. Peyton thinks for a moment and asks, "Can I try another pie?"

"I'm so proud of you, Peyton. Which pie do you want?"

"Chess pie, please. And do you think Uncle Sherwood might teach me some chess moves? Maybe I would like chess if I gave it another try."

Peter raises his glass and clinks it with a fork.
"Here's to pie. Especially pie à la mode."

Best-Ever Apple Pie

Serves 8

Prepare Ingredients

- 2 (12-inch) pie dough rounds*

- 2 pounds Golden Delicious, Fuji, or Jonagold apples, peeled, cored, and sliced ¼ inch thick

- 1½ pounds McIntosh, Cortland, or Empire apples, peeled, cored, and sliced ¼ inch thick

- 2 tablespoons all-purpose flour

- 1 teaspoon grated lemon zest plus 1 tablespoon juice, squeezed from ½ lemon

- ¼ teaspoon salt

- ⅛ teaspoon ground cinnamon

- ½ cup (3½ ounces) plus 1 teaspoon sugar, measured separately

- 1 large egg, lightly beaten

Gather Baking Equipment

- 9-inch pie plate
- Plastic wrap
- Rimmed baking sheet
- Aluminum foil
- Large microwave-safe bowl
- Rubber spatula
- Oven mitts
- Scissors
- Paring knife
- Pastry brush
- Cooling rack

Start Baking!

1. Carefully place 1 pie dough round in 9-inch pie plate. Gently press dough against bottom and sides of pie plate, letting excess hang over edge of plate. Cover pie plate loosely with plastic wrap and refrigerate until firm, about 30 minutes. Refrigerate second pie dough round until needed.

2. Adjust oven rack to lowest position and heat oven to 425 degrees. Line rimmed baking sheet with aluminum foil.

3. In large microwave-safe bowl, use rubber spatula to toss apples, flour, lemon zest, salt, cinnamon, and ½ cup sugar together. Heat apple mixture in microwave, stirring occasionally, until apples are slightly softened, about 5 minutes. Use oven mitts to remove bowl from microwave.

4. Stir lemon juice into apple mixture and let cool for 10 minutes. Spread apple mixture in chilled dough-lined pie plate, mounding apples slightly in middle.

5. Place chilled dough round over center of apple mixture. Use scissors to trim edge of dough ½ inch beyond edge of pie plate. Use your fingers to pinch edges of top and bottom crusts firmly together. Fold extra dough under itself onto rim of pie plate; folded edge should be flush with edge of plate. Use your fingers and knuckles to crimp edges of dough around pie.

6. Use paring knife to cut five 2-inch slits in top of dough. Use pastry brush to paint top of pie with beaten egg. Sprinkle evenly with remaining 1 teaspoon sugar.

7. Place pie on foil-lined baking sheet and place in oven. Bake until crust is light golden brown, about 25 minutes. Reduce oven temperature to 375 degrees and continue to bake until juices are bubbling and crust is deep golden brown, 30 to 35 minutes.

8. Use oven mitts to remove baking sheet from oven. Use oven mitts to transfer pie to cooling rack and let cool for at least 2 hours. Serve slightly warm or at room temperature.

*Roll 2 rounds of store-bought pie dough into 12-inch rounds or make homemade pie dough. See ATKkids.com/pie_dough for pie dough recipe.

Copyright © 2020 by America's Test Kitchen. Cover and interior illustrations by Michelle Mee Nutter. Design by Scott Murry. The characters and events portrayed in this book are fictitious or are used fictitiously. Any similarity to real persons, living or dead, is purely coincidental and not intended by the author. All rights reserved. No part of this book may be reproduced or transmitted in any manner whatsoever without written permission from the publisher, except in the base of brief quotations embedded in critical articles or reviews.

Library of Congress Cataloging-in-Publication Data
Names: Bishop, Jack, 1963- author. | Nutter, Michelle Mee, illustrator. | America's Test Kitchen (Firm)
Title: Peyton picks the perfect pie : a Thanksgiving celebration / story by Jack Bishop ; illustrations by Michelle Mee Nutter.
Description: Boston, MA : America's Test Kitchen, [2020] | Summary: Peyton knows her parents wish she were less particular about what she eats, so she decides to try pie when family and friends gather for Thanksgiving dinner—but which one? Includes a recipe for Best-Ever Apple Pie.
Identifiers: LCCN 2020003855 | ISBN 9781948703260 (hardcover)
Subjects: CYAC: Food habits—Fiction. | Pies—Fiction. | Family life—Fiction. | Thanksgiving Day—Fiction.
Classification: LCC PZ7.1.B549 Pey 2020 | DDC [E]—dc23
LC record available at https://lccn.loc.gov/2020003855

AMERICA'S TEST KITCHEN
21 Drydock Avenue, Boston, MA 02210

Manufactured in the United States of America
10 9 8 7 6 5 4 3 2 1

Distributed by Penguin Random House
Publisher Services